Unstinky

WITHDRAWN

BY ANDY RASH

ARTHUR A. LEVINE BOOKS 🏮 AN IMPRINT OF SCHOLASTIC INC.

Bud was a happy stinkbug
MOST of the time . . .

CONTEST!

because Bud always had to compete with the biggest stinkers ever:

P. U. Bottoms,   Lord Stinkington,   and The Fumigator!

And every time Bud tried to stink, something went wrong.

SMOKESTACK DEAD FISH DOG DOO FLOWERS

He always made GOOD smells.

OUTHOUSE   GYM SOCK   SOUR MILK   PINE TREE

BUG SPRAY   ROTTEN EGGS   ARM PIT   NEW CAR

Another big stinking failure! But Bud had an idea.

ONIONS!

MANURE!

A SKUNK!

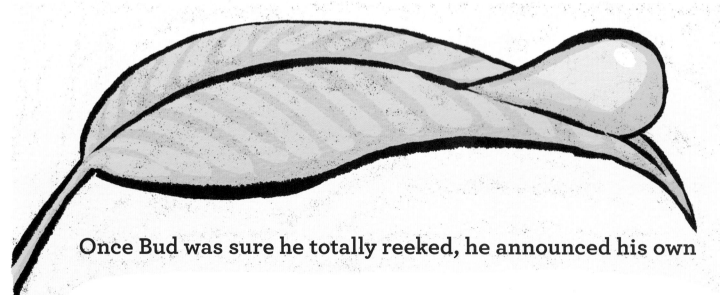

Once Bud was sure he totally reeked, he announced his own

STINKING CONTEST!

But as all the stinkbugs lined up . . .

. . . a big dewdrop fell!

SPLASH!

GARBAGE TRUCK

LIMBURGER CHEESE

BURNING WIG

FRESH-BAKED BREAD

Fourth place again.
Bud wandered off to mope . . .

. . . and ran into Major Funk, a stinkbug with a high rank.

"What's wrong, Bud?" Major Funk yelled.

"I can't stink, sir. I don't know how," said Bud.

"Nonsense!" yelled Major Funk. "Every stinkbug can stink! Just do what I do!"

"Stomp your feet!"

"Wave your arms!"

"Waggle your bottom!"

GUNPOWDER

CANDY CANE

Major Funk sniffed the air.
"Hmmm. Well, keep working on it,
Bud. You're sure to stink someday."

Bud did keep working on it. All day,
he stomped and waved and waggled.
He jumped and slid and twirled.

TULIP

DAISY

ROSE

GARDENIA

POPPY

DAFFODIL

VIOLET

PETUNIA

He flopped and reached and twitched.
But every smell that came out of him
was flowers, flowers, flowers.

A confused bee arrived.
"Hi, I'm April. Sorry to interrupt your dancing. I thought I smelled flowers."

"That flower smell is me," said Bud. "I'm trying to stink, but I'm no good at it."

"Maybe stinking just isn't your thing," said April. "But you sure can dance! Will you come with me to a dance party at the hive?"

"Do you think they'll even let me in?
I'm a stinkbug," said Bud.
"Don't be silly! They'll be happy to
see you!" said April.

The bees were NOT happy to see Bud, but the guards let him in because he was April's guest, and April was a V.I.B. (a very important bee).

Bud and April danced,

and danced,

and danced,

and danced!

And then . . .

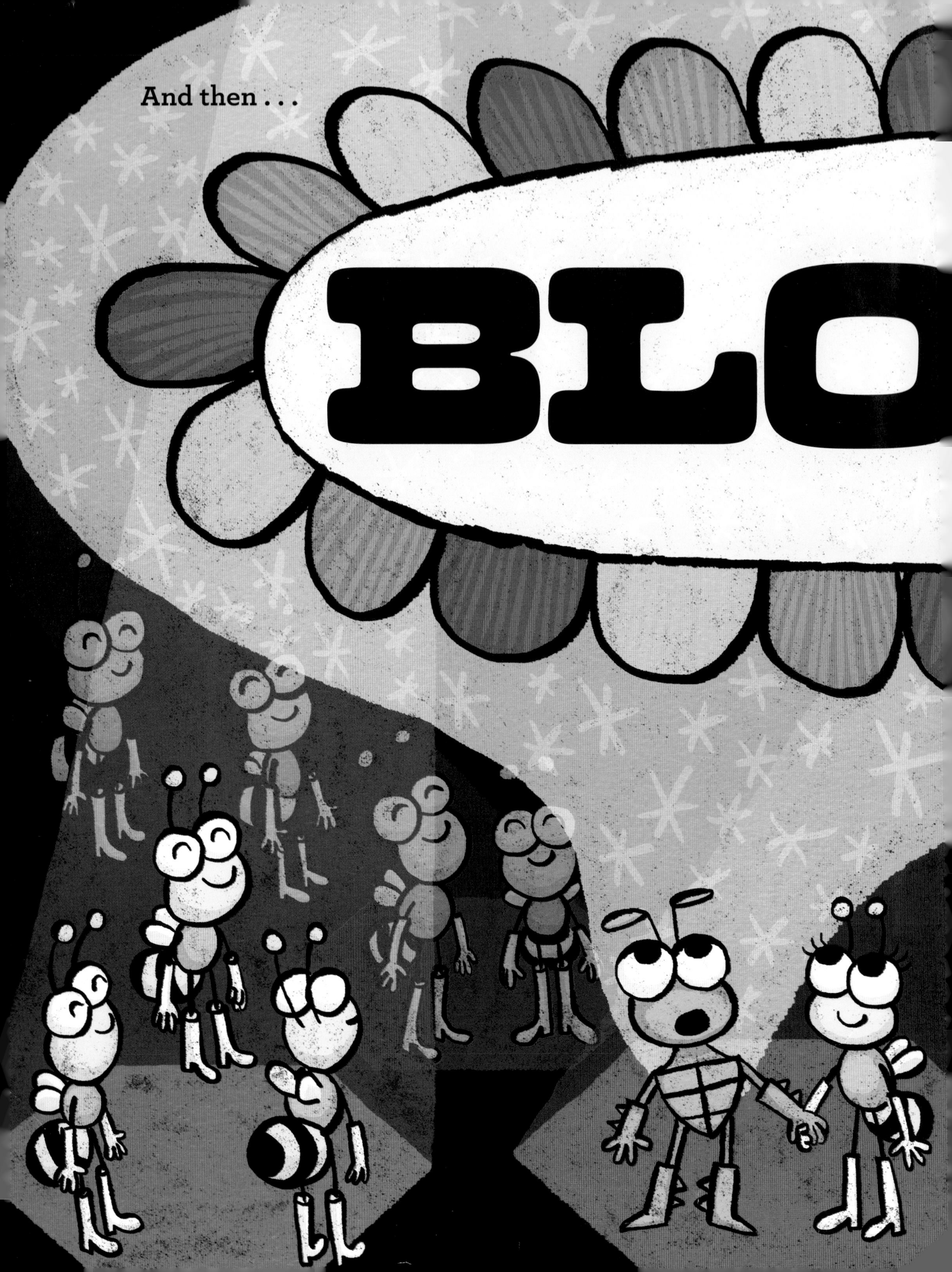

OM!

"Mmmmm!" hummed all of the bees.

Her Royal Majesty the Queen Bee arrived!
"Bud the stinkbug, you have graced this hive
with your dancing and aroma. You are always a
welcome guest."

"Hooray!" said all of the bees.

Bud went back and told his friends about dancing. They had never heard of it.

They gave it a shot, but it clearly wasn't their thing.

VOLCANO

CHEESE FACTORY

DINOSAUR POO

Although the exercise improved their stinking quite a bit.
They thanked Bud as he said good-bye . . .

... and Bud went back to do his thing.

For Joe and Katie

Library of Congress Control Number: 2017058735

ISBN 978-0-439-36880-3
10 9 8 7 6 5 4 3 2 1   18 19 20 21 22
Printed in China 62
First edition, October 2018

The illustrations for this book are a combination of gouache, ink, and digital techniques.
Book design by Andy Rash and Charles Kreloff